KT-449-243

For Jess, Helen, Katie and Synthia *R L S*

For Roger *T K*

First published in Great Britain in 2005
by Orion Children's Books
This paperback edition first published in 2006
by Orion Children's Books
a division of the Orion Publishing Group Ltd
Orion House
5 Upper St Martin's Lane
London WC2H 9EA

Text © Ruth Louise Symes 2005
Illustrations © Tony Kenyon 2005

A catalogue record for this book is available from the British Library.

Printed in Italy.

ISBN-10 1 84255 513 8
ISBN-13 978 184255 513 2

www.orionbooks.co.uk

'The lessons in forming relationships are obvious yet beautifully hidden . . . Tony Kenyon's illustrations, detailed, almost realistic but subtly asserting the different characters of the rabbits are finely done and a good complement to the story.' *Carousel*

Praise for *Floppy Ears*, the first story about Floppy Ears, Twitchy Nose and Little Tail:

'A gentle story with a very positive message for young children.'
The Bookseller

'A heartwarming tale, with charming illustrations and some acute observations.' *Junior Magazine*

Little Tail

Story by Ruth Louise Symes

Illustrations by Tony Kenyon

Orion
Children's Books

Twitchy Nose and Floppy Ears were playing school when there was a knock at the door.

'Who can this be?' said Mum.

Outside stood a big rabbit and a little rabbit.
'We came to say hello,' the big rabbit said.
'Hello,' said Mum. 'Won't you come in?'

And the big rabbit and the little rabbit did.

'Would you like some carrot tops?' said Mum.
'Yes, please,' said the big rabbit.

'What's your name?' the little rabbit whispered to Floppy Ears.
'Floppy Ears,' said Floppy Ears. 'What's yours?'
'Little Tail,' said the little rabbit.
'My name's Twitchy Nose,' said Twitchy Nose.

Little Tail and
Floppy Ears played
hide and seek

and chasing

and tickling.

Twitchy Nose didn't.

When Floppy Ears and Little Tail were too tired to play
any more Little Tail's mum said: 'We'd better be going now.'
'Can I play with Floppy Ears tomorrow?' said Little Tail.
'Please, please.'

'Of course, if Floppy Ears would like to,' said Little Tail's mum.
'I'd like to!' said Floppy Ears.

'Where's Floppy Ears?' asked Sneezer, when
Twitchy Nose went out to play the next day.
'Floppy Ears has a new friend,' Twitchy Nose said.

'That's good,' said Bendy Whiskers.
'Yes, now I won't have somebody following
me around all the time!' said Twitchy Nose.

At first Floppy Ears and Little Tail played happily together,

chasing butterflies

and jumping over sticks

and making daisy chains.

But then they didn't.
'That's my carrot!' said Floppy Ears.
'I saw it first,' said Little Tail.
'No you didn't!' said Floppy Ears.

'Ouch!' said Floppy Ears.   'Ouch!' said Little Tail.

'I don't like you any more,' said Floppy Ears.
'And I don't like you. Not one little bit,' said Little Tail.

'I don't ever want to speak to you again,' said Floppy Ears.
'And I don't ever want to speak to you either,' said Little Tail.

'I'm going to play by myself,' said Floppy Ears.
'And I'm going to play by myself,' said Little Tail.

Twitchy Nose saw Floppy Ears all alone.
'Where's Little Tail?' Twitchy Nose asked.

'I don't know,' said Floppy Ears.

'Hello, Little Tail, not playing with
Floppy Ears any more?' said Sneezer.

'No,' said Little Tail.

Twitchy Nose didn't like Floppy Ears
and Little Tail not being friends.
  'Why don't you play with Little Tail?'
Twitchy Nose said to Floppy Ears.
  'We can't play together because we're
not friends any more,' said Floppy Ears.

'We have to do something,' Twitchy Nose said to
Sneezer and Bendy Whiskers. 'We have to make
Floppy Ears and Little Tail friends again.'
   'But what can we do?' said Sneezer.

'I know,' said Twitchy Nose.

Twitchy Nose raced home

and came back holding two carrots.

'One for you.
And one for you,'
said Twitchy Nose.

'Do you want to be my friend again?' said Floppy Ears.
'Yes please,' said Little Tail.

'I did it, they're friends again!' said Twitchy Nose
to Sneezer and Bendy Whiskers.

'Come on. Let's play racing.
I'm very good at racing.'

Twitchy Nose kept on racing all the way home.

That night Twitchy Nose said: 'Are you going to play with Little Tail again tomorrow?'

'Yes,' said Floppy Ears. 'But I don't know what game to play.'

'I know,' said Twitchy Nose.

'Let's play school.'

And they did.